First published in Belgium and Holland by Clavis Uitgeverij, Hasselt – Amsterdam, 2015
Copyright © 2015, Clavis Uitgeverij
English translation from the Dutch by Clavis Publishing Inc. New York
Copyright © 2016 for the English language edition: Clavis Publishing Inc. New York
Visit us on the web at www.clavisbooks.com

On a Journey written and illustrated by Guido van Genechten
Original title: *Op reis*
Translated from the Dutch by Clavis Publishing

ISBN 978-1-60537-276-1

This book was printed in December 2015 at SOCIETA' EDITORIALE GRAFICHE AZ s.r.l.
Viale del Lavoro, 8 - 37036 S. Martino Buon Albergo (VR) – Italy

First Edition
10 9 8 7 6 5 4 3 2 1

For all my travel companions

GUIDO
VAN
GENECHTEN

ON A JOURNEY

Clavis

NEW YORK

www.clavisbooks.com

Frog had never been outside his own little village.
Until the day his friend Hedgehog came by and asked:
"Are you coming with me?"
"Where to?" Frog wanted to know.
"On a journey," Hedgehog said.
"On a journey?" asked Frog.
"Yes," Hedgehog said, "jump in the back seat."

NEAR ROAD

FAR ROAD

"Are you sitting comfortably?" Hedgehog asked.
"Please put your seatbelt on."
Frog nodded and fastened his seatbelt.
His friend started the car.
"Here we go," he said, "wave goodbye."

They left Frog's little village.

"We are going on a journey!" Frog cheered.
"We are on a journey," Hedgehog said.

"Being on a journey is fun!" said Frog.

"The wind is blowing around my ears, and the sun is shining on my nose.
I feel as free as a..."

"As a frog?" Hedgehog smiled.

"Ha-ha, free as a frog; that's a good one!" His green friend giggled in the back seat.

After a while, Frog asked: "So? Are we there yet?"
"We are on a journey, Frog," answered Hedgehog.

They drove, for hours.

At the foot of High Mountain Frog asked:

"Do we have to go all the way up?"

"Of course," Hedgehog said, "that's where the road goes."

"Oh," said Frog.

HIGH MOUNTAIN

They drove uphill for a while.

"Are we there yet?" Frog asked again.

Hedgehog kept his eyes on the road.

In the distance dark, rain-filled clouds were gathering.

With a press of the button Hedgehog closed the folding roof.

"Are we almost there?" Frog tried again.

"Listen," Hedgehog said, "to how the rain is pattering on the roof."

At the top Hedgehog turned off the engine.
He opened the folding roof,
breathed in the fresh mountain air,
and looked around for several minutes.
Finally he sighed with delight and said:
"Beautiful, just beautiful."
"Nice," Frog nodded. "So this is it then?"
"Not really." Hedgehog shook his head.
"We are on a journey, remember?"

THE VALLEY
THE TOP

They drove on. For days.

"Look," Hedgehog said, "we're going to drive into a tunnel. Isn't this exciting?"

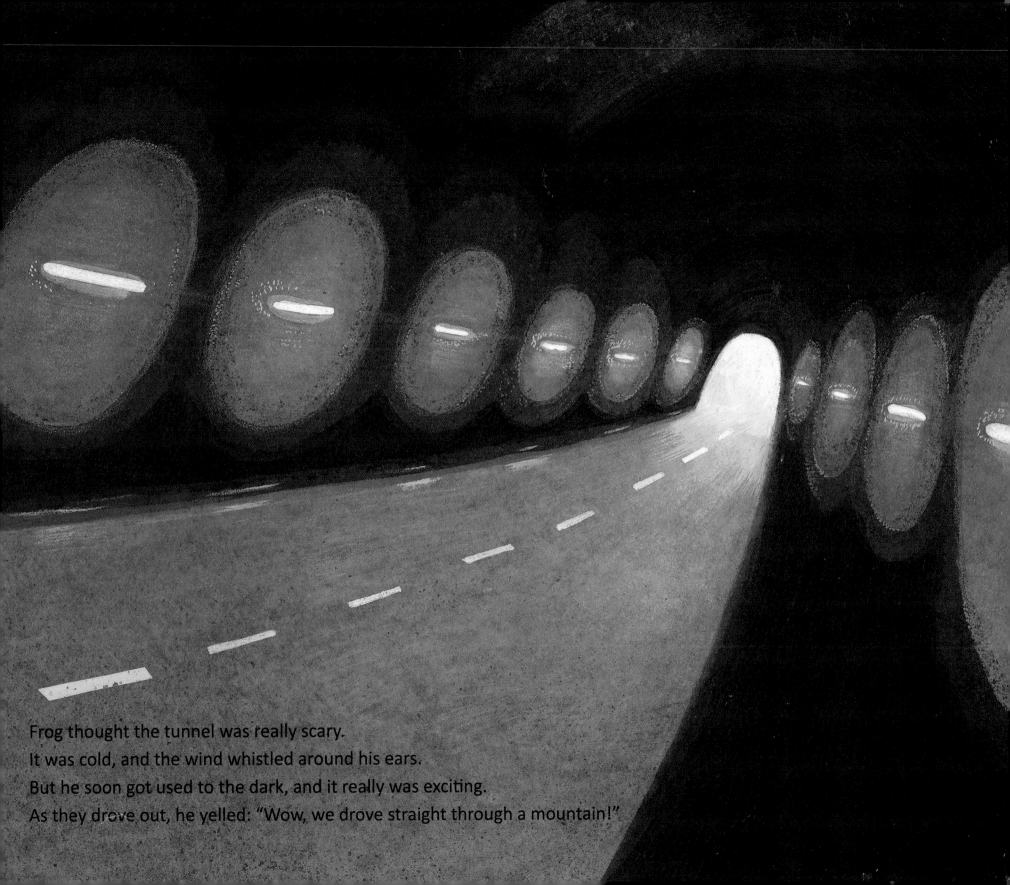

Frog thought the tunnel was really scary.

It was cold, and the wind whistled around his ears.

But he soon got used to the dark, and it really was exciting.

As they drove out, he yelled: "Wow, we drove straight through a mountain!"

"Hey!" Frog cried. "We are driving over water, and up there, cars are hanging from a rope. And over there in the distance, all that glistening blue... What could that be?"
"That's the sea," Hedgehog told him.

"Beautiful..." was all Frog could say when they were looking at the sea together.
He'd never known there were places where you could look so far.
"Can we go any further?" Frog asked.

"Of course," Hedgehog said. "We are on a *journey*, aren't we?"

Carefully Hedgehog drove the car onto a ferry. It took them all the way to the other side.

They drove off the boat. And then they drove on. For weeks.

Along the way they listened to stories they'd never heard.

They ate exotic fruits, tasted all sorts of delicious food,

and listened to music so beautiful it almost made them cry.

By then Frog had learned how to drive.
One day they arrived back at Frog's little village,
which they had left months ago.
Frog stopped. "Wow! Everything has changed around here," he said.
Hedgehog looked at his friend and smiled.
"You have changed, too, Frog," he said.

That made Frog think.

NEAR ROAD

FAR ROAD